STRANGER THINGS

SIX #2

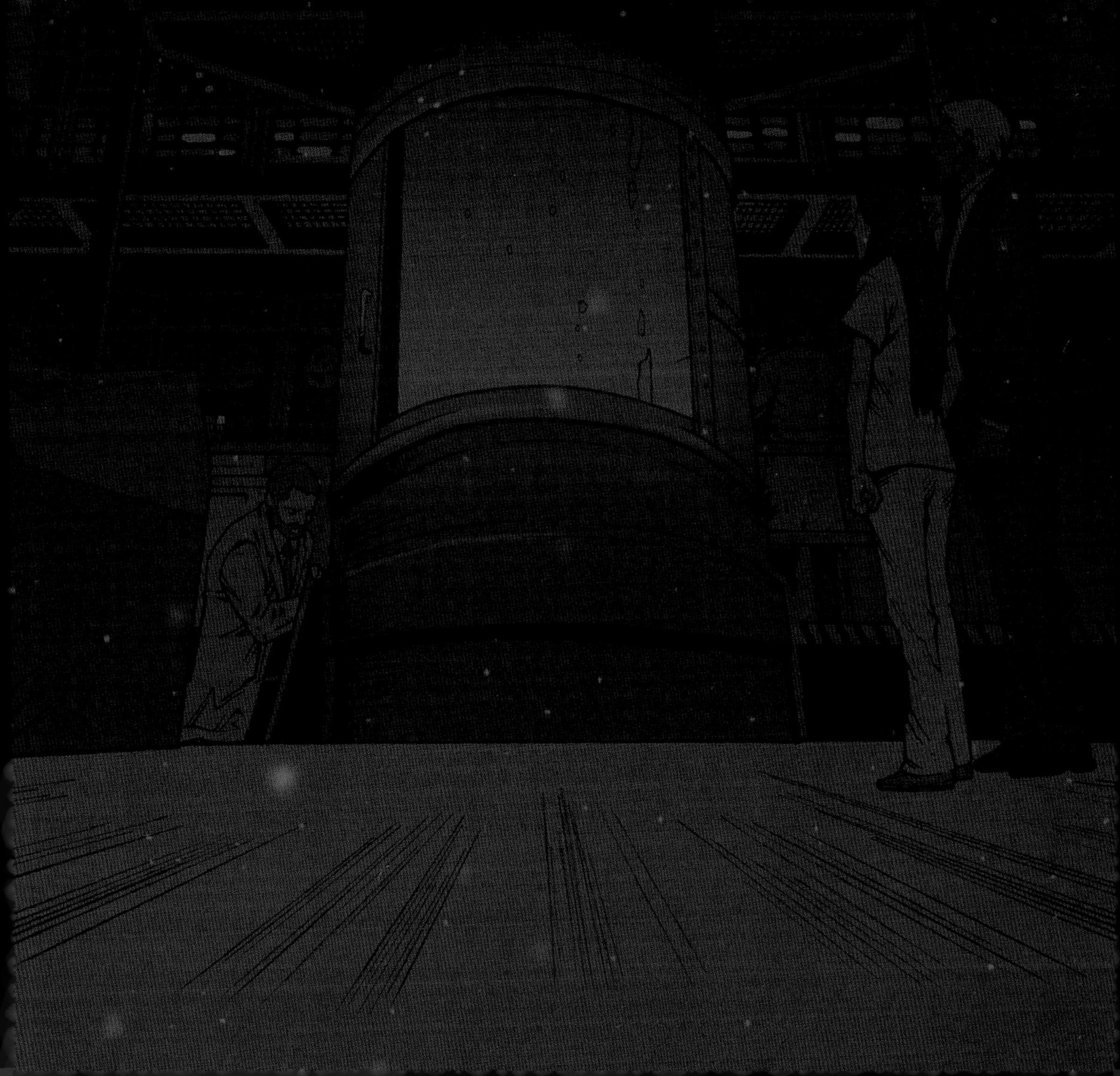

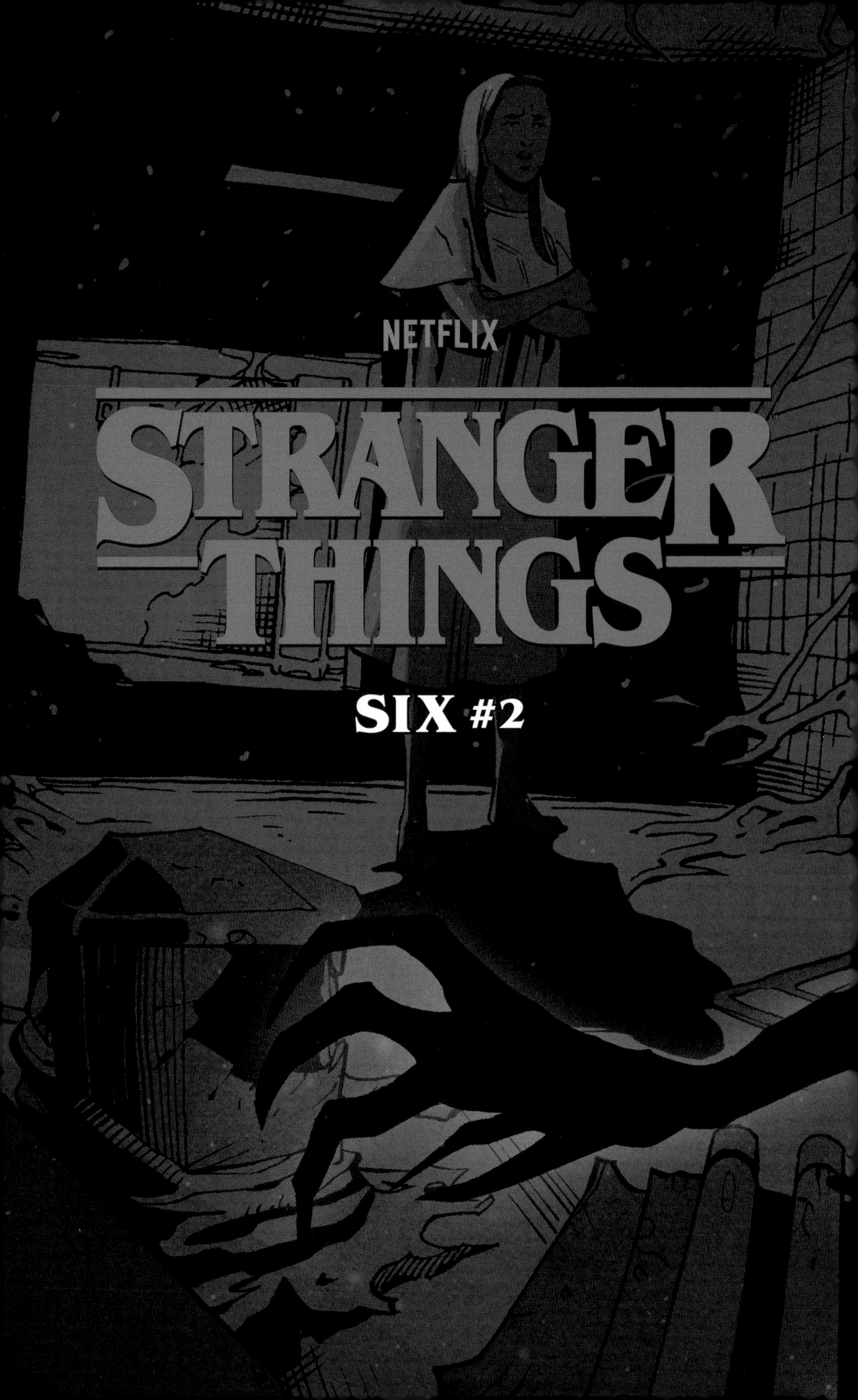
NETFLIX
STRANGER
THINGS
SIX #2

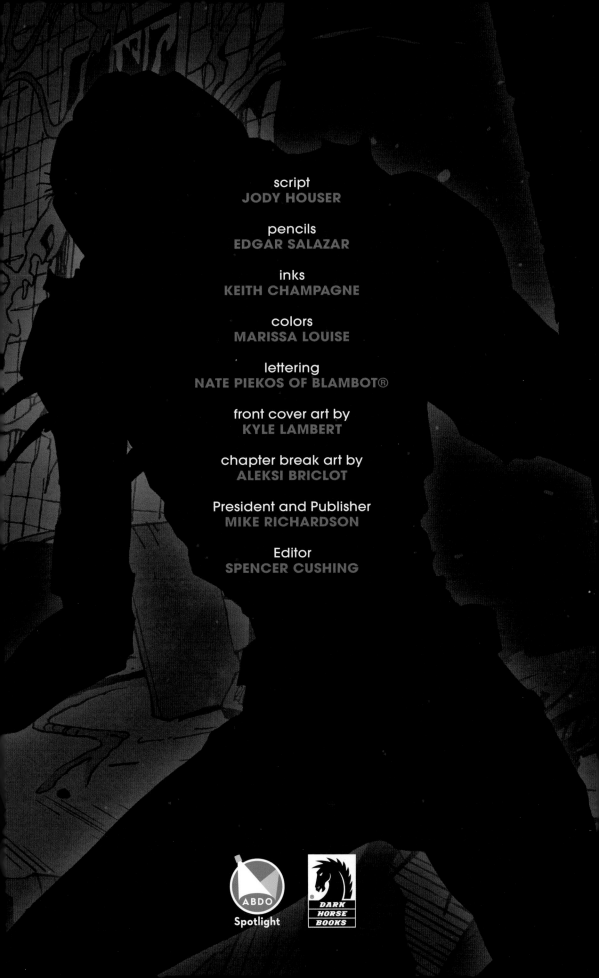

script
JODY HOUSER

pencils
EDGAR SALAZAR

inks
KEITH CHAMPAGNE

colors
MARISSA LOUISE

lettering
NATE PIEKOS OF BLAMBOT®

front cover art by
KYLE LAMBERT

chapter break art by
ALEKSI BRICLOT

President and Publisher
MIKE RICHARDSON

Editor
SPENCER CUSHING

ABDO
Spotlight

DARK
HORSE
BOOKS

ABDOBOOKS.COM

Reinforced library bound edition published in 2020 by Spotlight, a division of ABDO, PO Box 398166, Minneapolis, Minnesota 55439. Spotlight produces high-quality reinforced library bound editions for schools and libraries.
Published by agreement with Dark Horse Comics.

Printed in the United States of America, North Mankato, Minnesota.
092019
012020

THIS BOOK CONTAINS RECYCLED MATERIALS

DARK HORSE BOOKS

NETFLIX
OFFICIAL MERCHANDISE
©NETFLIX

Library of Congress Control Number: 2019942387

Publisher's Cataloging-in-Publication Data

Names: Houser, Jody, author. | Salazar, Edgar; Champagne, Keith; Louise, Marissa; Piekos, Nate, illustrators.
Title: Six / by Jody Houser; illustrated by Edgar Salazar; Keith Champagne; Marissa Louise; Nate Piekos.
Description: Minneapolis, Minnesota : Spotlight, 2020 | Series: Stranger things
Summary: A teenage girl with precognitive abilities ends up as the pawn of a government agency that wants to harness her powers for its own ends.
Identifiers: ISBN 9781532144400 (#1, lib. bdg.) | ISBN 9781532144417 (#2, lib. bdg.) | ISBN 9781532144424 (#3, lib. bdg.) | ISBN 9781532144431 (#4, lib. bdg.)
Subjects: LCSH: Stranger things (Television program)--Juvenile fiction. | Science fiction television programs--Juvenile fiction. | Supernatural disappearances--Juvenile fiction. | Monsters--Juvenile fiction. | Graphic novels--Juvenile fiction. | Comic books, strips, etc.--Juvenile fiction.
Classification: DDC 741.5--dc23

ABDO
Spotlight

A Division of ABDO
abdobooks.com

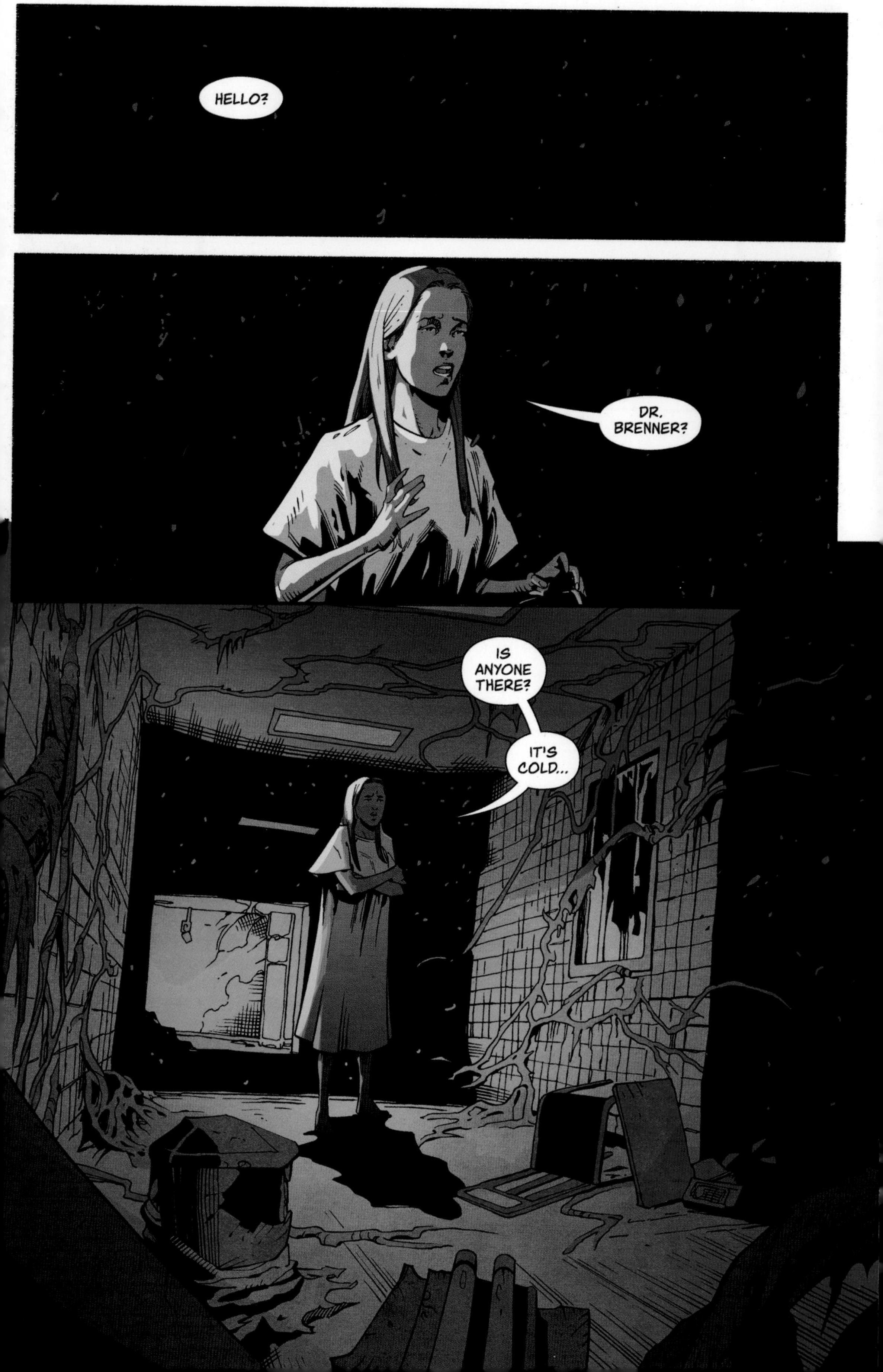
HELLO?
DR. BRENNER?
IS ANYONE THERE?
IT'S COLD...

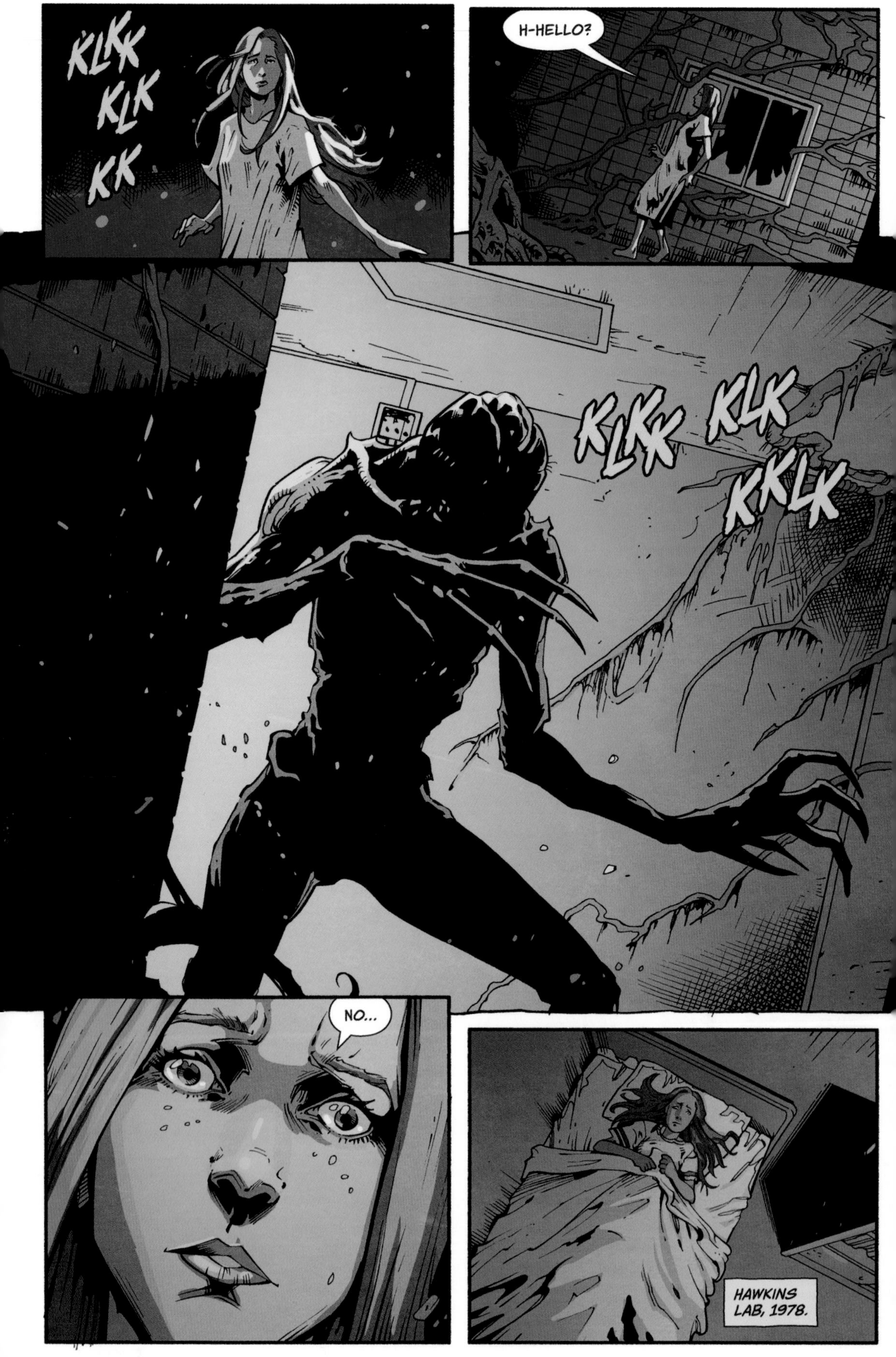
KLKK
KLK
KK
H-HELLO?
KLKK KLK
KKLK
NO...
HAWKINS LAB, 1978.

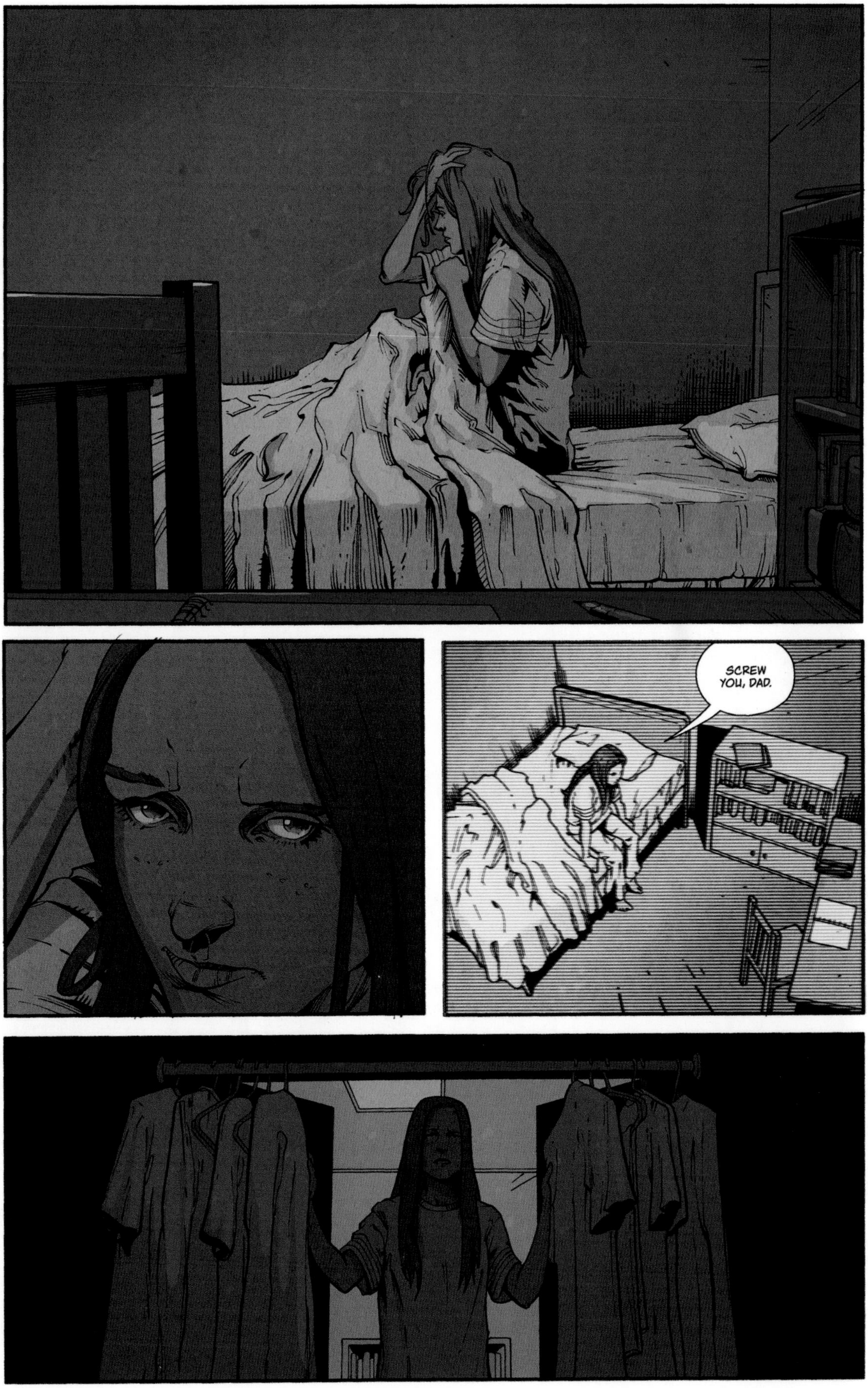
SCREW YOU, DAD.

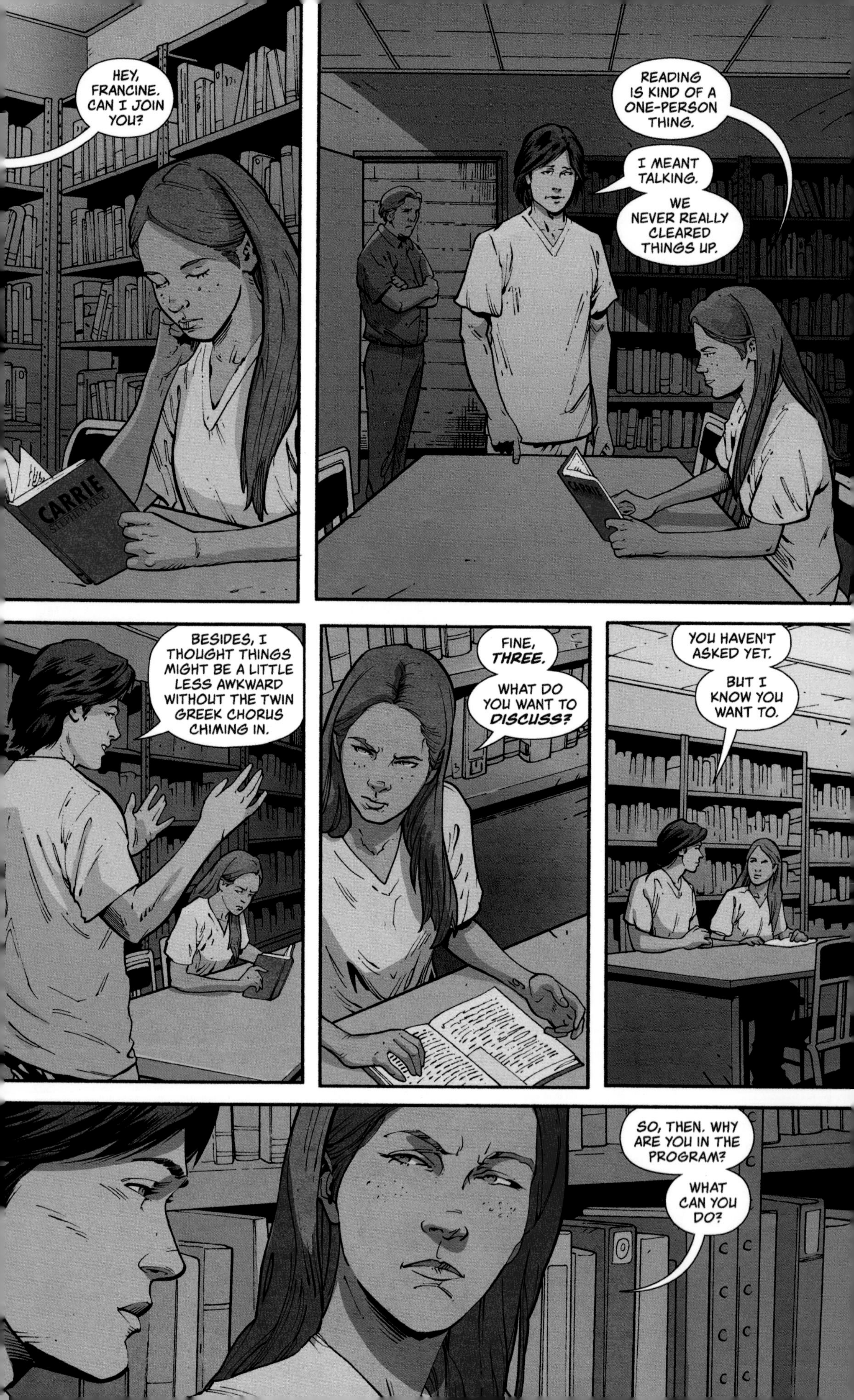
HEY, FRANCINE. CAN I JOIN YOU?
CARRIE
STEPHEN KING
READING IS KIND OF A ONE-PERSON THING.
I MEANT TALKING.
WE NEVER REALLY CLEARED THINGS UP.
BESIDES, I THOUGHT THINGS MIGHT BE A LITTLE LESS AWKWARD WITHOUT THE TWIN GREEK CHORUS CHIMING IN.
FINE, *THREE.*
WHAT DO YOU WANT TO *DISCUSS?*
YOU HAVEN'T ASKED YET.
BUT I KNOW YOU WANT TO.
SO, THEN. WHY ARE YOU IN THE PROGRAM?
WHAT CAN YOU DO?

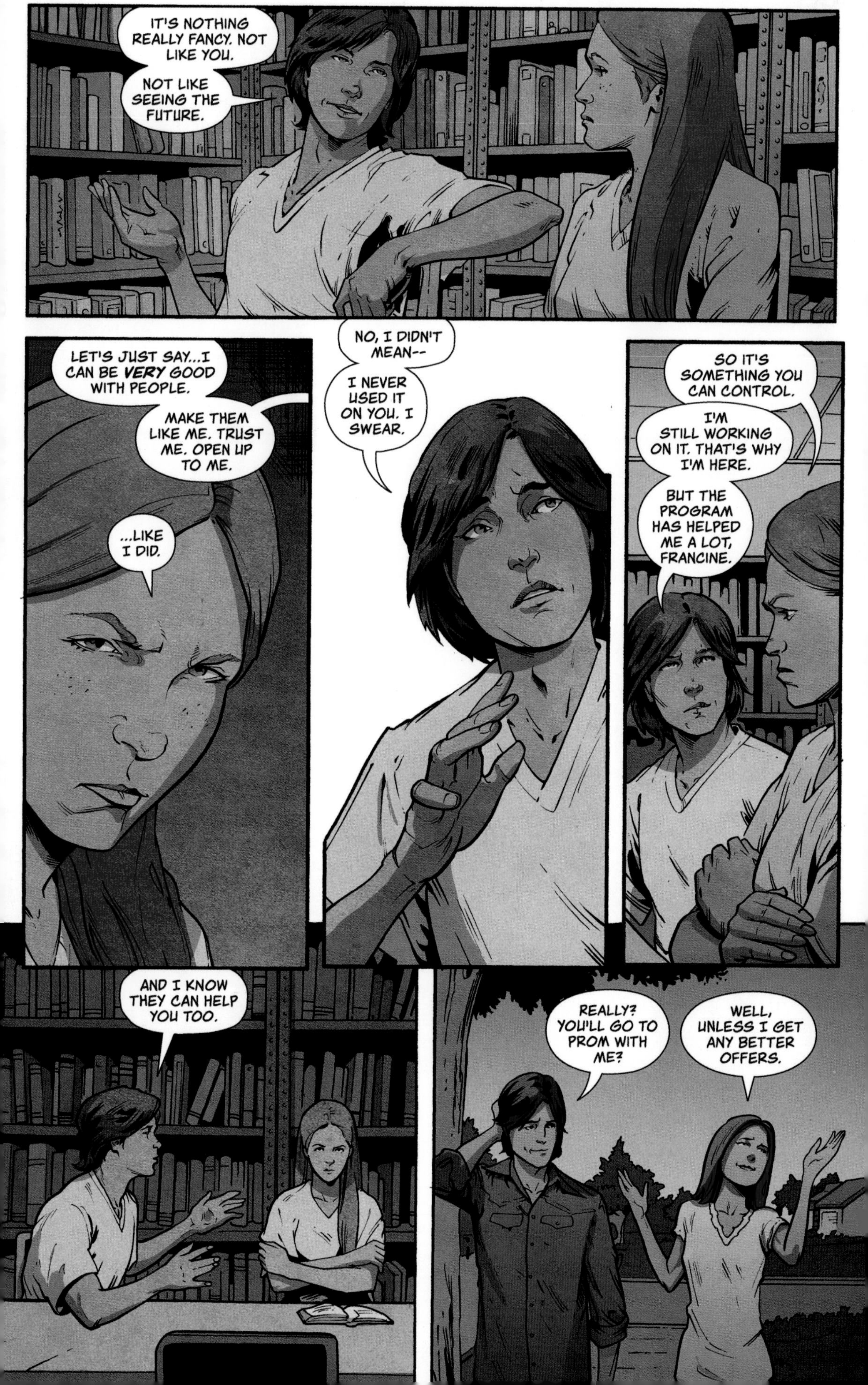
IT'S NOTHING REALLY FANCY. NOT LIKE YOU.
NOT LIKE SEEING THE FUTURE.
LET'S JUST SAY...I CAN BE *VERY* GOOD WITH PEOPLE.
MAKE THEM LIKE ME. TRUST ME. OPEN UP TO ME.
...LIKE I DID.
NO, I DIDN'T MEAN--
I NEVER USED IT ON YOU. I SWEAR.
SO IT'S SOMETHING YOU CAN CONTROL.
I'M STILL WORKING ON IT. THAT'S WHY I'M HERE.
BUT THE PROGRAM HAS HELPED ME A LOT, FRANCINE.
AND I KNOW THEY CAN HELP YOU TOO.
REALLY? YOU'LL GO TO PROM WITH ME?
WELL, UNLESS I GET ANY BETTER OFFERS.

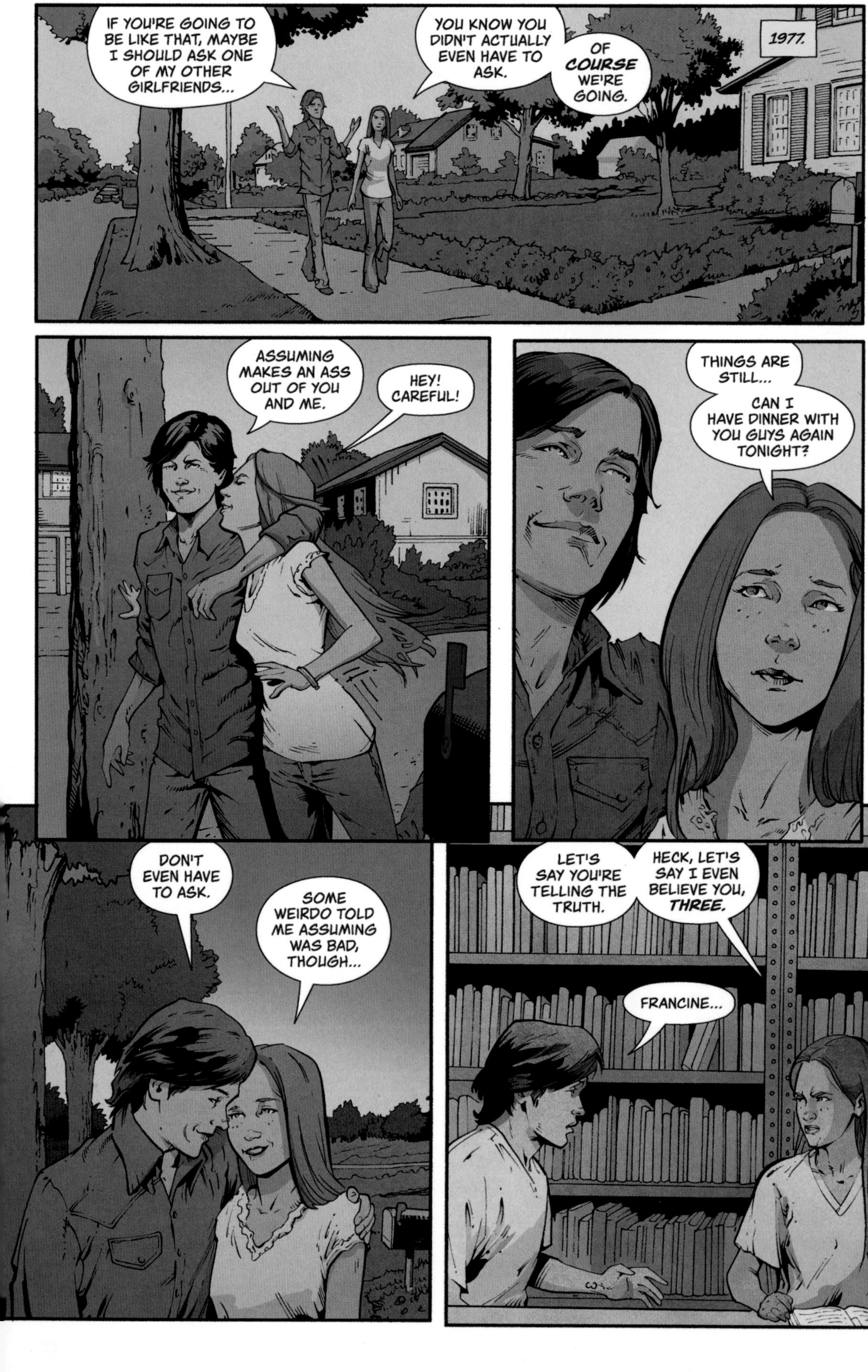
1977.
IF YOU'RE GOING TO BE LIKE THAT, MAYBE I SHOULD ASK ONE OF MY OTHER GIRLFRIENDS...
YOU KNOW YOU DIDN'T ACTUALLY EVEN HAVE TO ASK.
OF COURSE WE'RE GOING.
ASSUMING MAKES AN ASS OUT OF YOU AND ME.
HEY! CAREFUL!
THINGS ARE STILL...
CAN I HAVE DINNER WITH YOU GUYS AGAIN TONIGHT?
DON'T EVEN HAVE TO ASK.
SOME WEIRDO TOLD ME ASSUMING WAS BAD, THOUGH...
LET'S SAY YOU'RE TELLING THE TRUTH.
HECK, LET'S SAY I EVEN BELIEVE YOU, THREE.
FRANCINE...

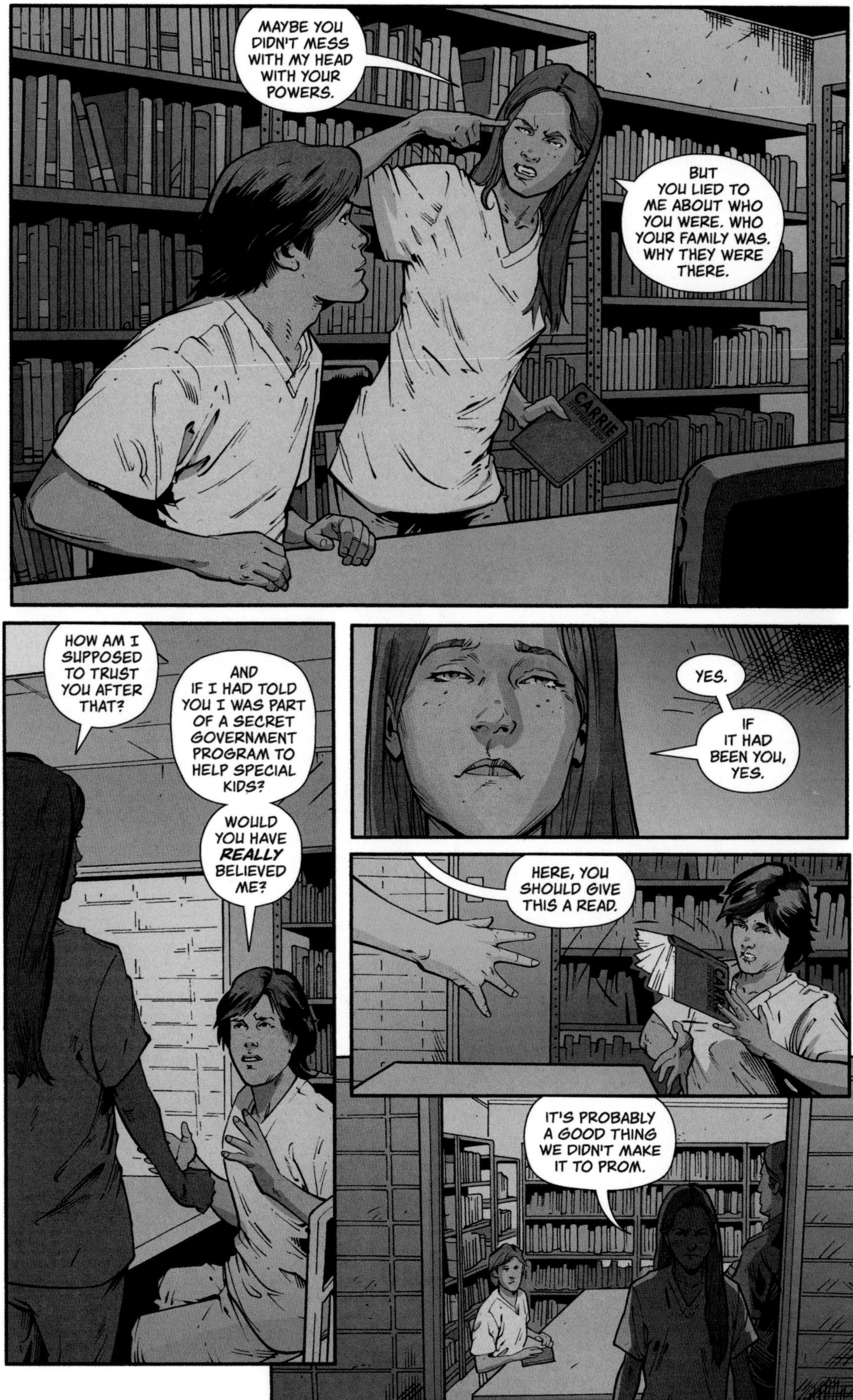
MAYBE YOU DIDN'T MESS WITH MY HEAD WITH YOUR POWERS.
BUT YOU LIED TO ME ABOUT WHO YOU WERE. WHO YOUR FAMILY WAS. WHY THEY WERE THERE.
CARRIE
STEPHEN KING
HOW AM I SUPPOSED TO TRUST YOU AFTER THAT?
AND IF I HAD TOLD YOU I WAS PART OF A SECRET GOVERNMENT PROGRAM TO HELP SPECIAL KIDS?
WOULD YOU HAVE *REALLY* BELIEVED ME?
YES.
IF IT HAD BEEN YOU, YES.
HERE, YOU SHOULD GIVE THIS A READ.
IT'S PROBABLY A GOOD THING WE DIDN'T MAKE IT TO PROM.

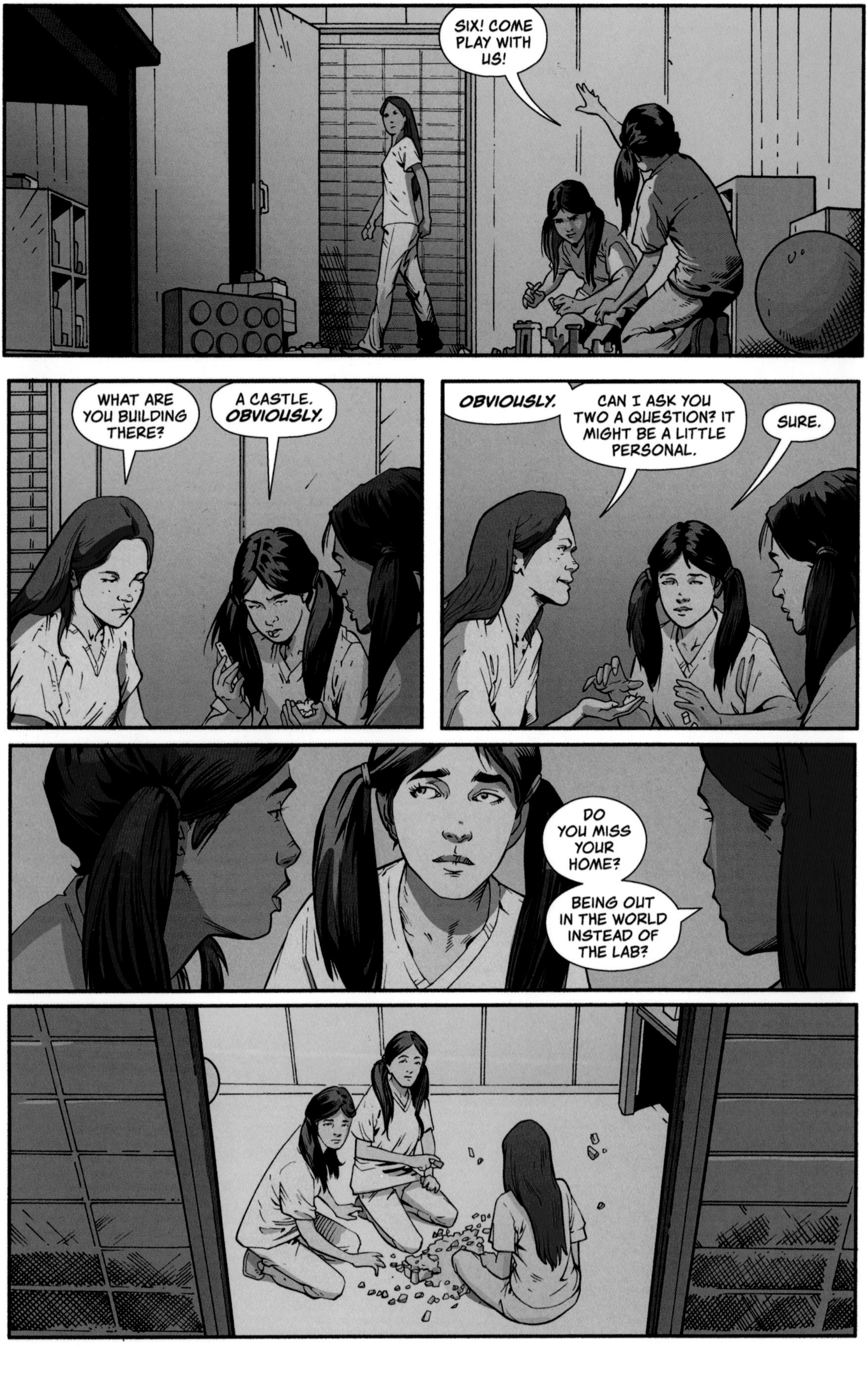
SIX! COME PLAY WITH US!
WHAT ARE YOU BUILDING THERE?
A CASTLE. *OBVIOUSLY.*
OBVIOUSLY.
CAN I ASK YOU TWO A QUESTION? IT MIGHT BE A LITTLE PERSONAL.
SURE.
DO YOU MISS YOUR HOME?
BEING OUT IN THE WORLD INSTEAD OF THE LAB?

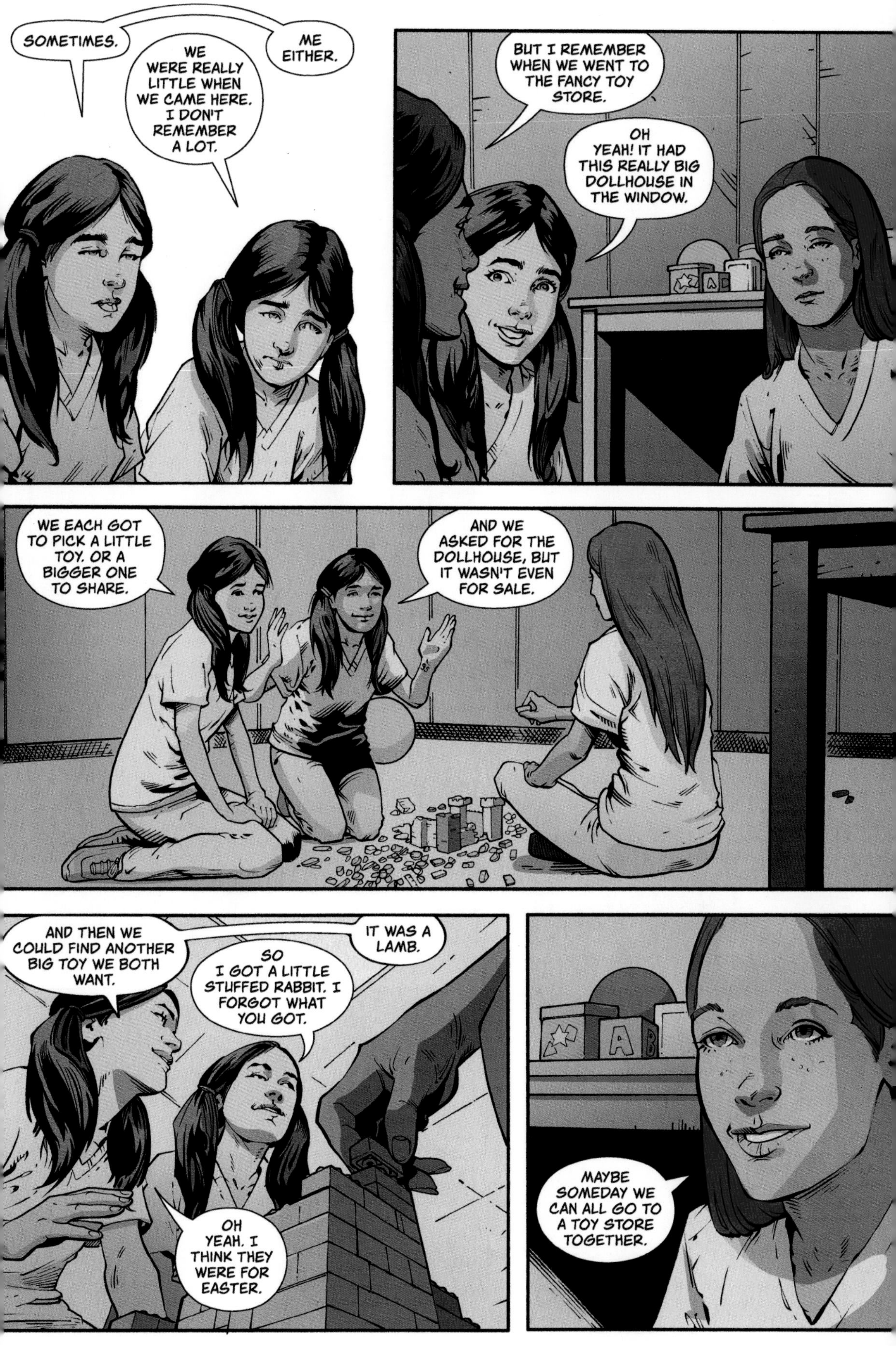
SOMETIMES.
WE WERE REALLY LITTLE WHEN WE CAME HERE. I DON'T REMEMBER A LOT.
ME EITHER.
BUT I REMEMBER WHEN WE WENT TO THE FANCY TOY STORE.
OH YEAH! IT HAD THIS REALLY BIG DOLLHOUSE IN THE WINDOW.
WE EACH GOT TO PICK A LITTLE TOY. OR A BIGGER ONE TO SHARE.
AND WE ASKED FOR THE DOLLHOUSE, BUT IT WASN'T EVEN FOR SALE.
AND THEN WE COULD FIND ANOTHER BIG TOY WE BOTH WANT.
SO I GOT A LITTLE STUFFED RABBIT. I FORGOT WHAT YOU GOT.
IT WAS A LAMB.
OH YEAH. I THINK THEY WERE FOR EASTER.
MAYBE SOMEDAY WE CAN ALL GO TO A TOY STORE TOGETHER.

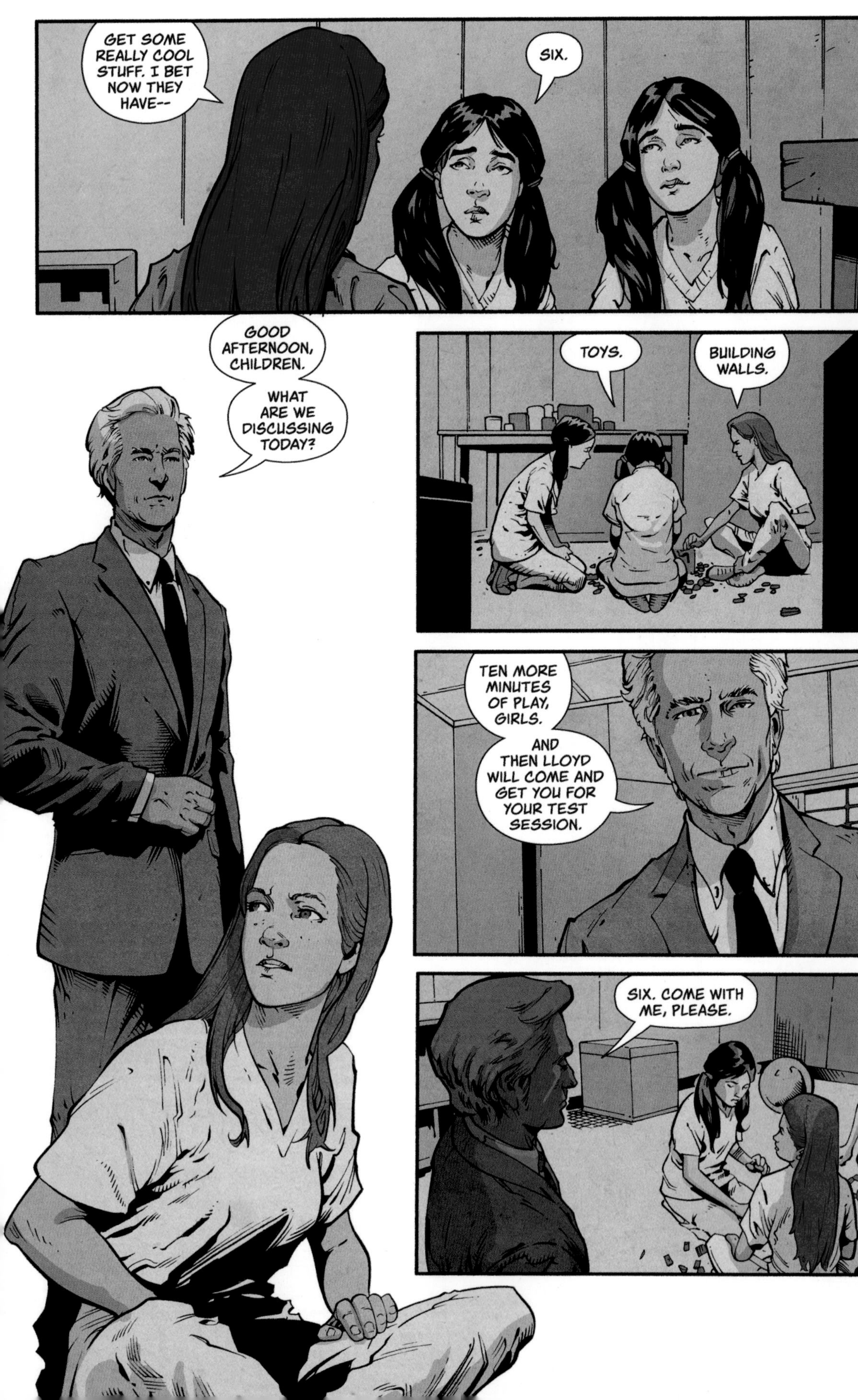
GET SOME REALLY COOL STUFF. I BET NOW THEY HAVE--
SIX.
GOOD AFTERNOON, CHILDREN.
WHAT ARE WE DISCUSSING TODAY?
TOYS.
BUILDING WALLS.
TEN MORE MINUTES OF PLAY, GIRLS.
AND THEN LLOYD WILL COME AND GET YOU FOR YOUR TEST SESSION.
SIX. COME WITH ME, PLEASE.

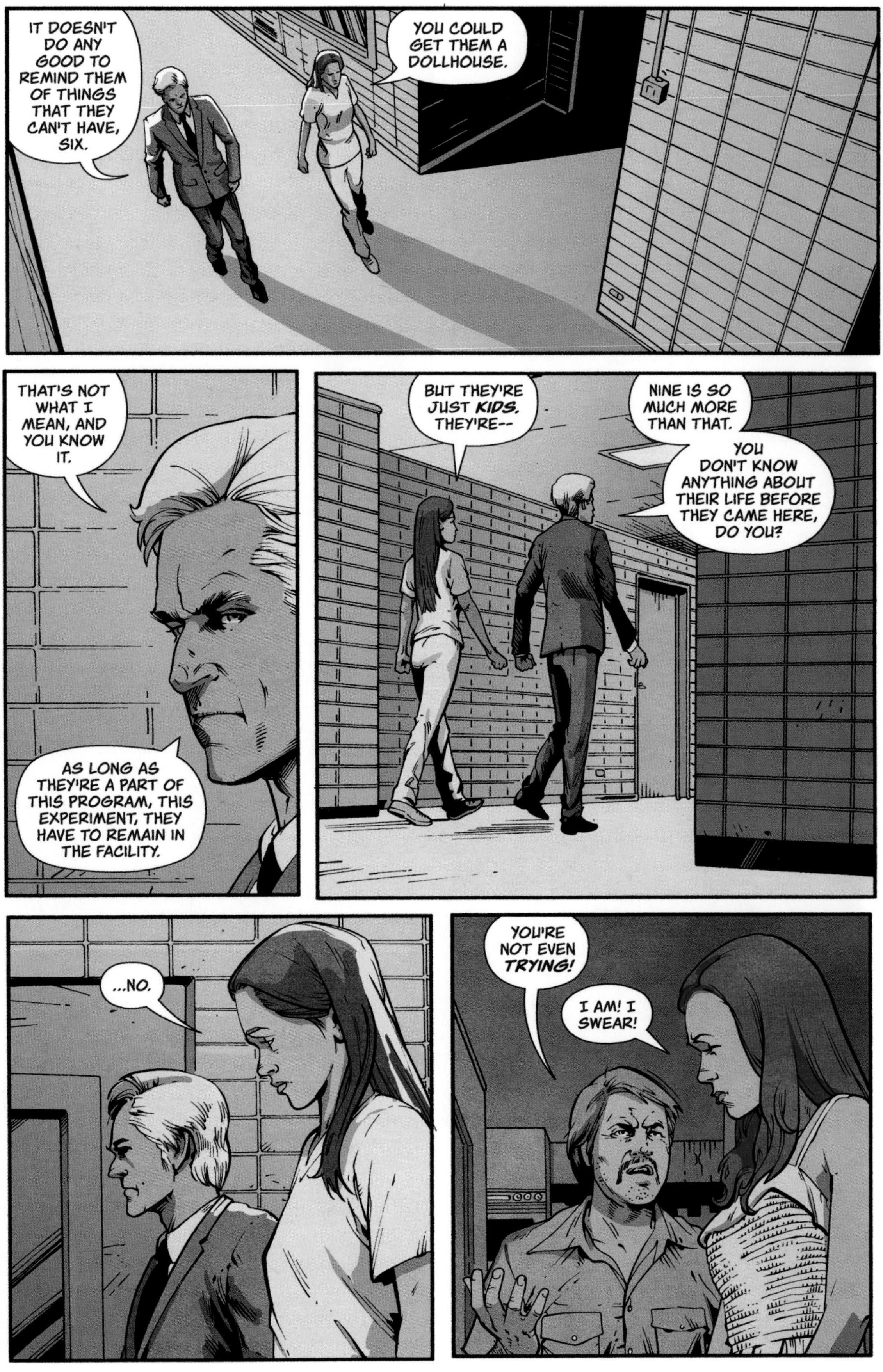
IT DOESN'T DO ANY GOOD TO REMIND THEM OF THINGS THAT THEY CAN'T HAVE, SIX.
YOU COULD GET THEM A DOLLHOUSE.
THAT'S NOT WHAT I MEAN, AND YOU KNOW IT.
AS LONG AS THEY'RE A PART OF THIS PROGRAM, THIS EXPERIMENT, THEY HAVE TO REMAIN IN THE FACILITY.
BUT THEY'RE JUST KIDS, THEY'RE--
NINE IS SO MUCH MORE THAN THAT.
YOU DON'T KNOW ANYTHING ABOUT THEIR LIFE BEFORE THEY CAME HERE, DO YOU?
...NO.
YOU'RE NOT EVEN TRYING!
I AM! I SWEAR!

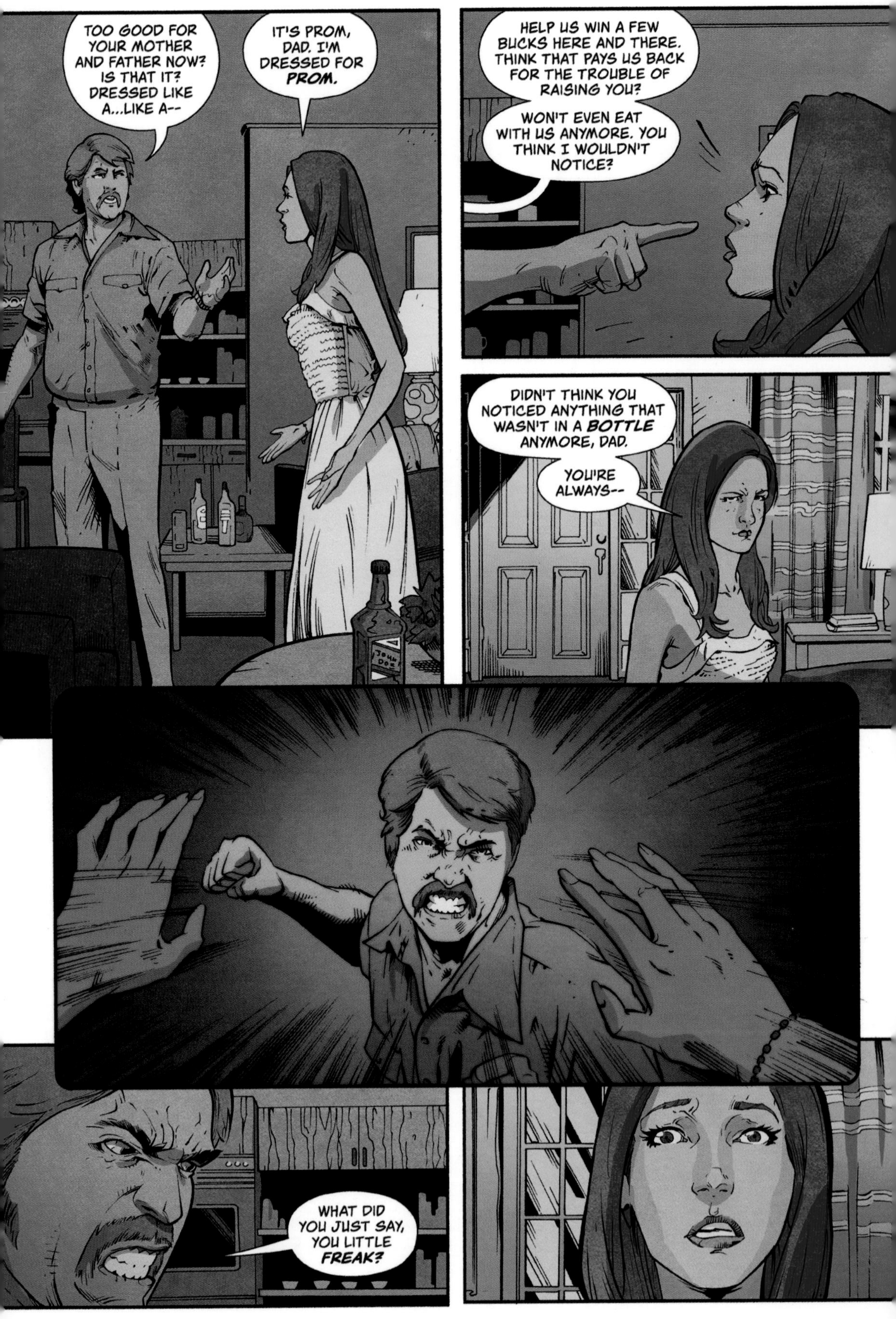
TOO GOOD FOR YOUR MOTHER AND FATHER NOW? IS THAT IT? DRESSED LIKE A...LIKE A--
IT'S PROM, DAD. I'M DRESSED FOR *PROM.*
HELP US WIN A FEW BUCKS HERE AND THERE. THINK THAT PAYS US BACK FOR THE TROUBLE OF RAISING YOU?
WON'T EVEN EAT WITH US ANYMORE. YOU THINK I WOULDN'T NOTICE?
DIDN'T THINK YOU NOTICED ANYTHING THAT WASN'T IN A *BOTTLE* ANYMORE, DAD.
YOU'RE ALWAYS--
WHAT DID YOU JUST SAY, YOU LITTLE *FREAK?*

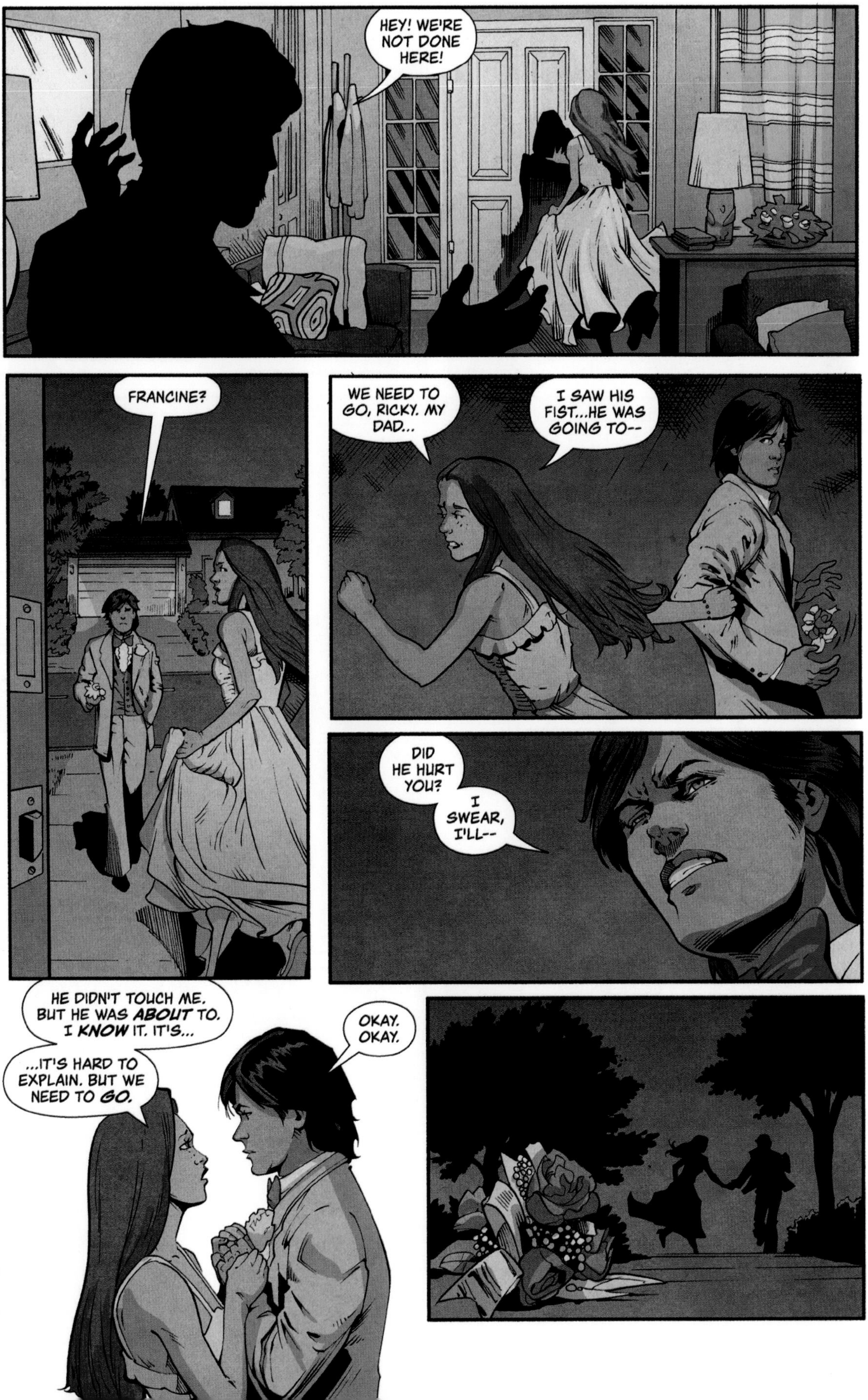
HEY! WE'RE NOT DONE HERE!
FRANCINE?
WE NEED TO GO, RICKY. MY DAD...
I SAW HIS FIST...HE WAS GOING TO--
DID HE HURT YOU?
I SWEAR, I'LL--
HE DIDN'T TOUCH ME. BUT HE WAS ABOUT TO. I KNOW IT. IT'S...
...IT'S HARD TO EXPLAIN. BUT WE NEED TO GO.
OKAY. OKAY.

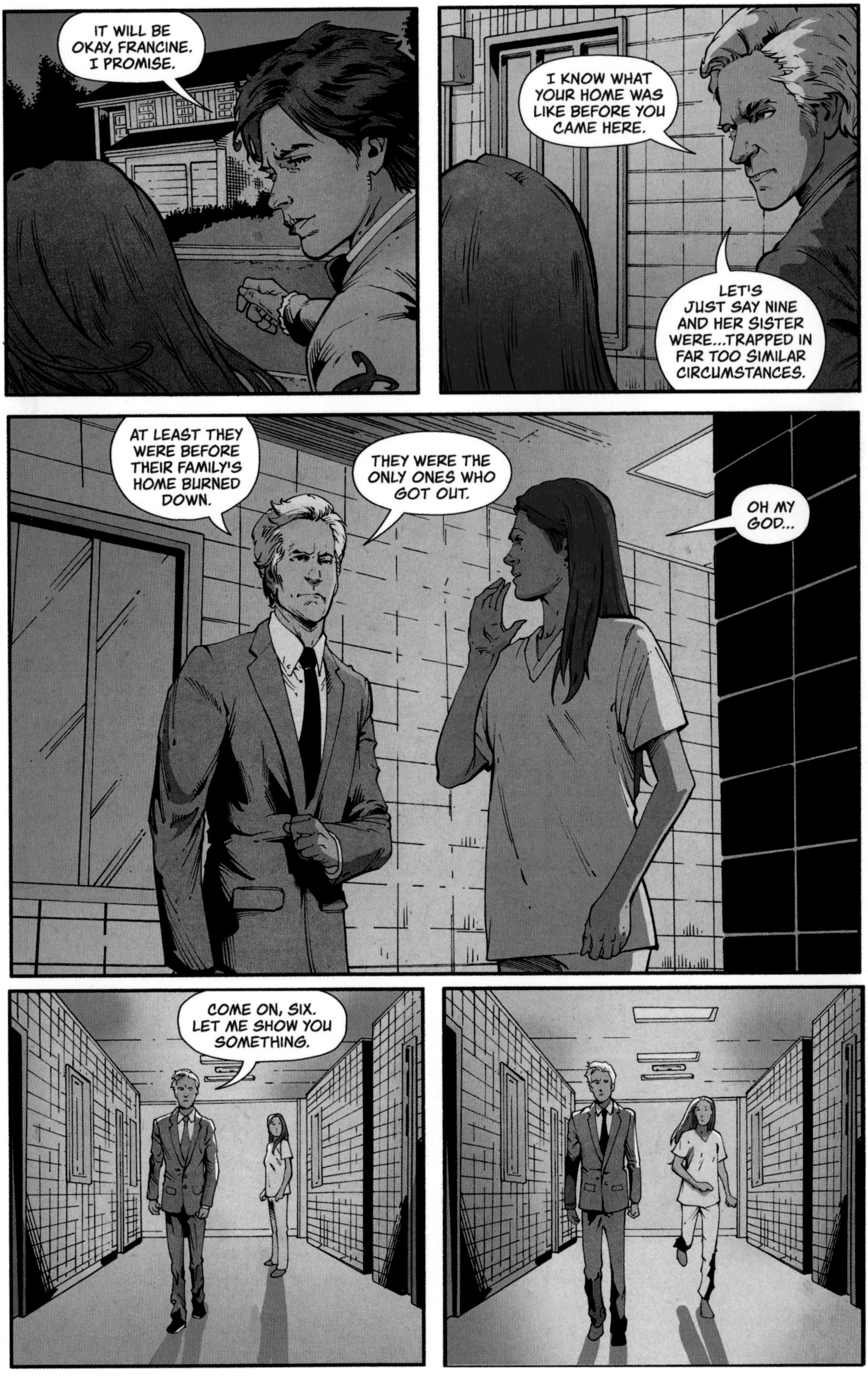
IT WILL BE OKAY, FRANCINE. I PROMISE.
I KNOW WHAT YOUR HOME WAS LIKE BEFORE YOU CAME HERE.
LET'S JUST SAY NINE AND HER SISTER WERE...TRAPPED IN FAR TOO SIMILAR CIRCUMSTANCES.
AT LEAST THEY WERE BEFORE THEIR FAMILY'S HOME BURNED DOWN.
THEY WERE THE ONLY ONES WHO GOT OUT.
OH MY GOD...
COME ON, SIX. LET ME SHOW YOU SOMETHING.

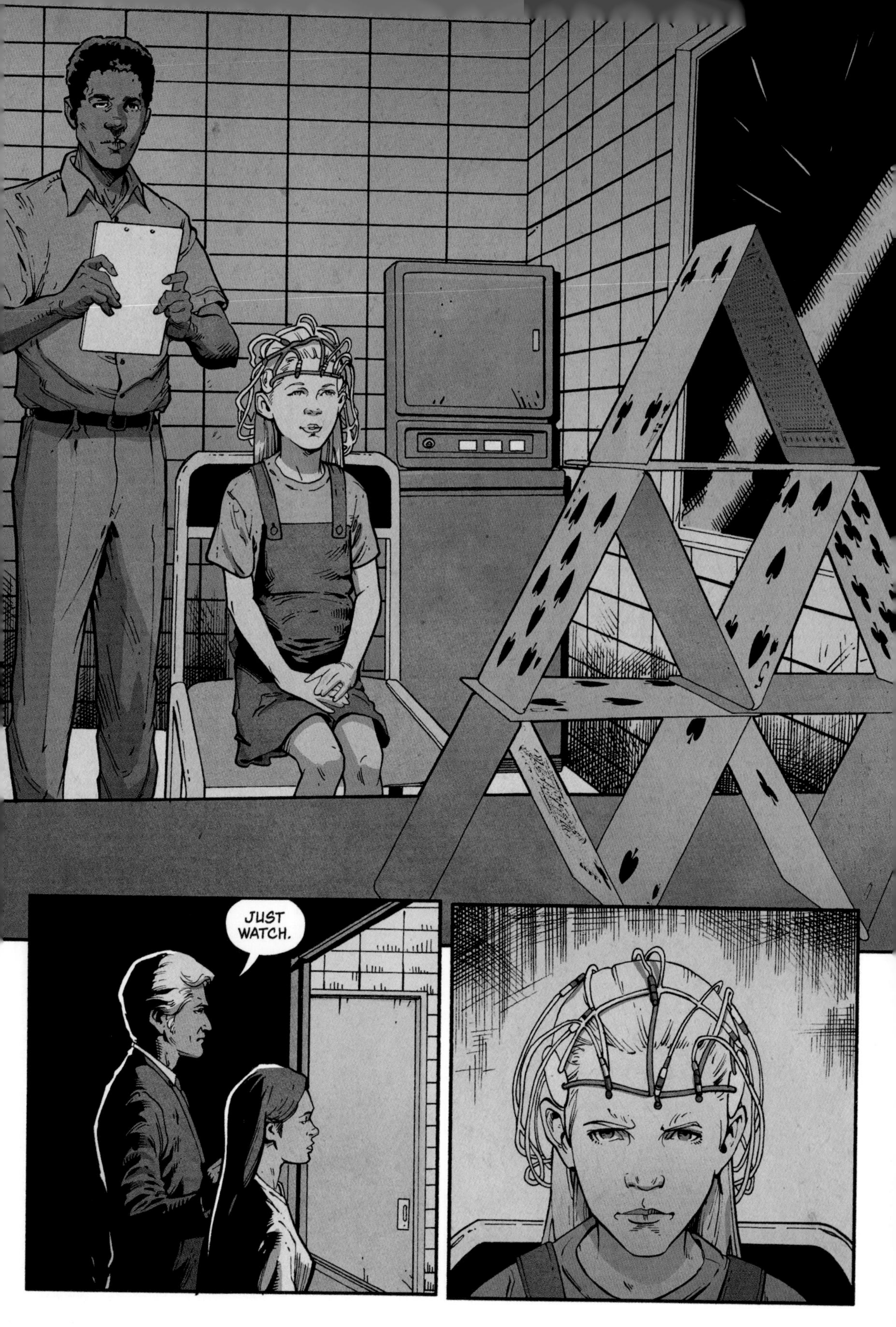
JUST WATCH.

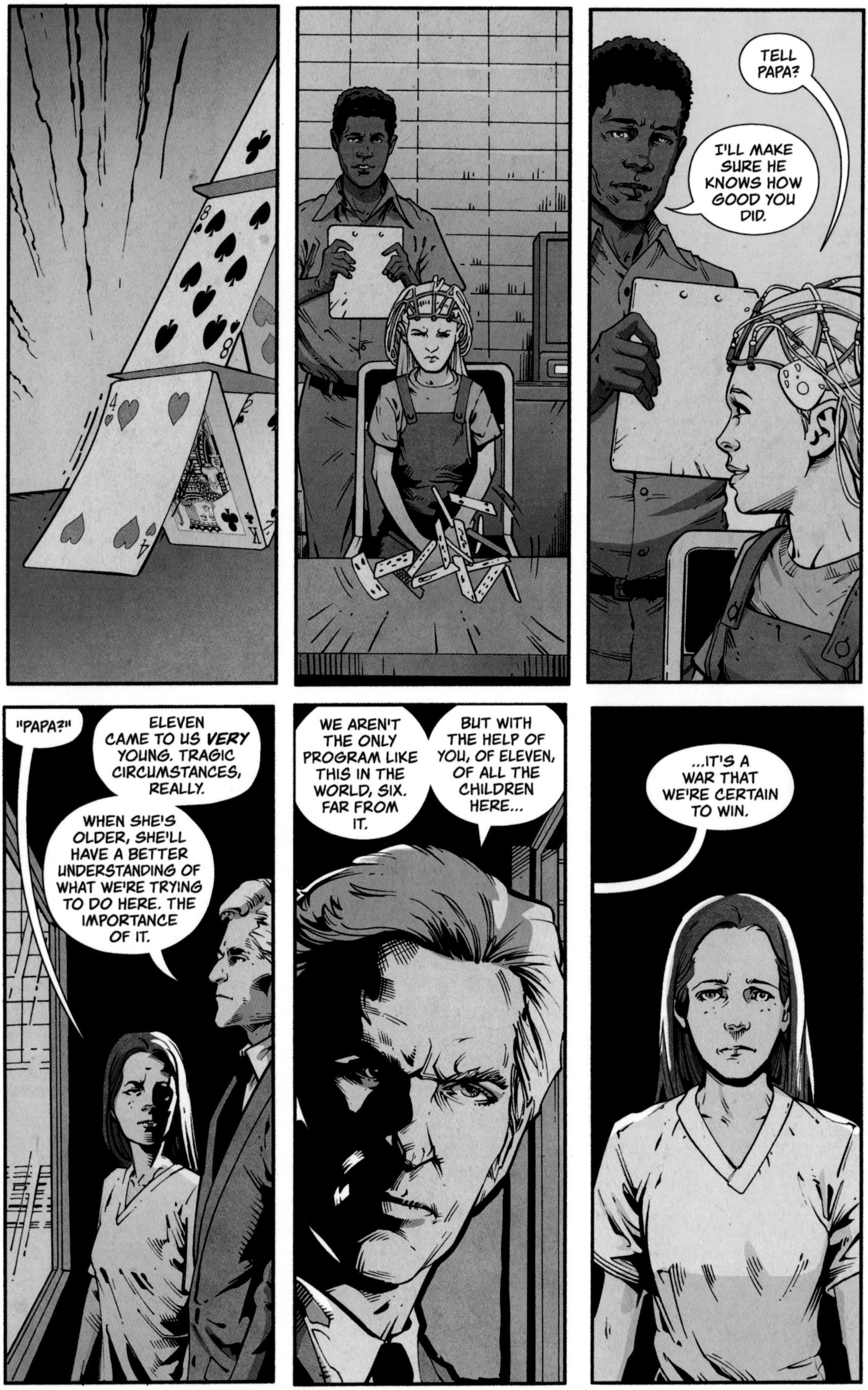
TELL PAPA?
I'LL MAKE SURE HE KNOWS HOW GOOD YOU DID.
"PAPA?"
ELEVEN CAME TO US VERY YOUNG. TRAGIC CIRCUMSTANCES, REALLY.
WHEN SHE'S OLDER, SHE'LL HAVE A BETTER UNDERSTANDING OF WHAT WE'RE TRYING TO DO HERE. THE IMPORTANCE OF IT.
WE AREN'T THE ONLY PROGRAM LIKE THIS IN THE WORLD, SIX. FAR FROM IT.
BUT WITH THE HELP OF YOU, OF ELEVEN, OF ALL THE CHILDREN HERE...
...IT'S A WAR THAT WE'RE CERTAIN TO WIN.

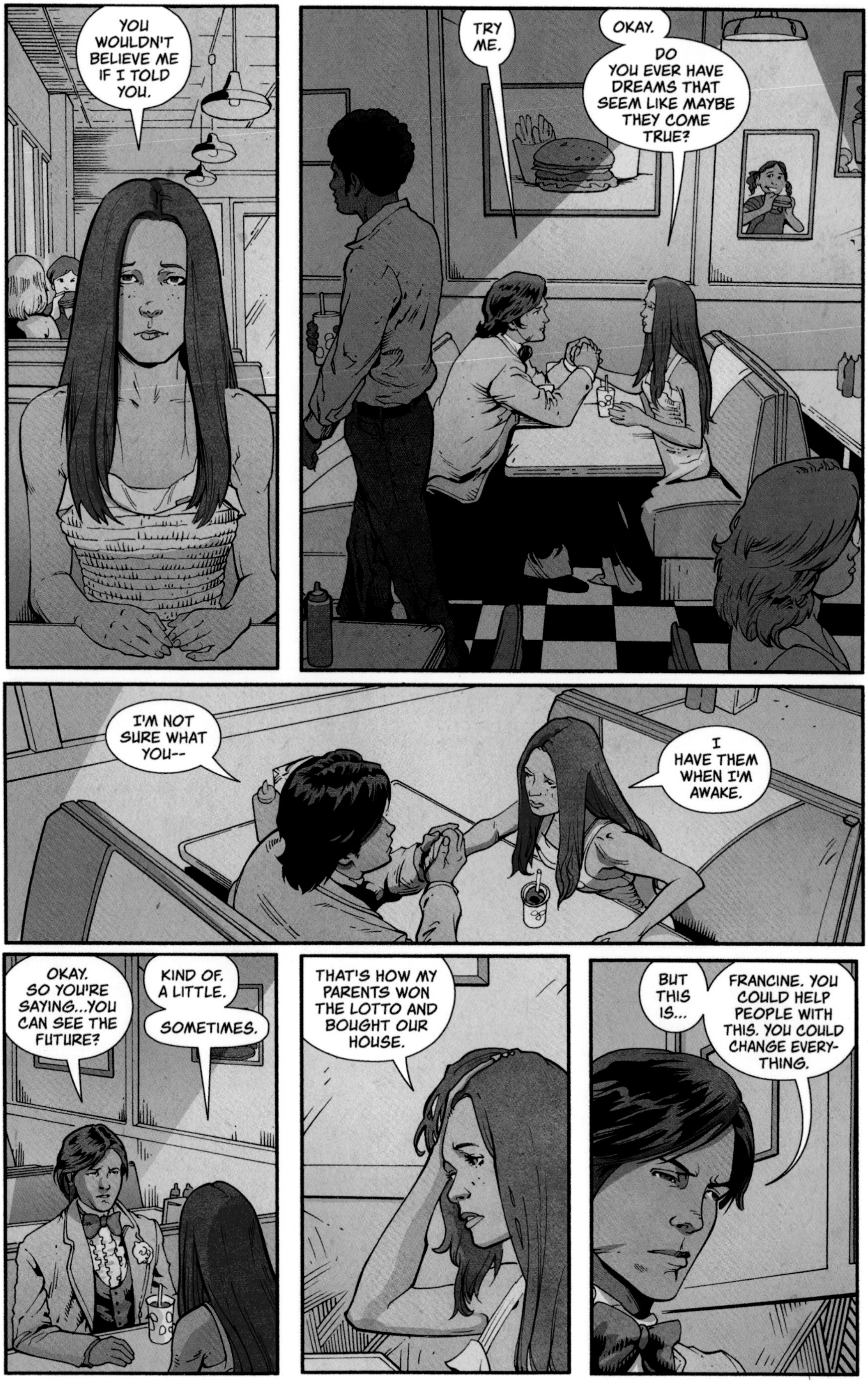
YOU WOULDN'T BELIEVE ME IF I TOLD YOU.
TRY ME.
OKAY.
DO YOU EVER HAVE DREAMS THAT SEEM LIKE MAYBE THEY COME TRUE?
I'M NOT SURE WHAT YOU--
I HAVE THEM WHEN I'M AWAKE.
OKAY. SO YOU'RE SAYING...YOU CAN SEE THE FUTURE?
KIND OF. A LITTLE.
SOMETIMES.
THAT'S HOW MY PARENTS WON THE LOTTO AND BOUGHT OUR HOUSE.
BUT THIS IS...
FRANCINE. YOU COULD HELP PEOPLE WITH THIS. YOU COULD CHANGE EVERY-THING.

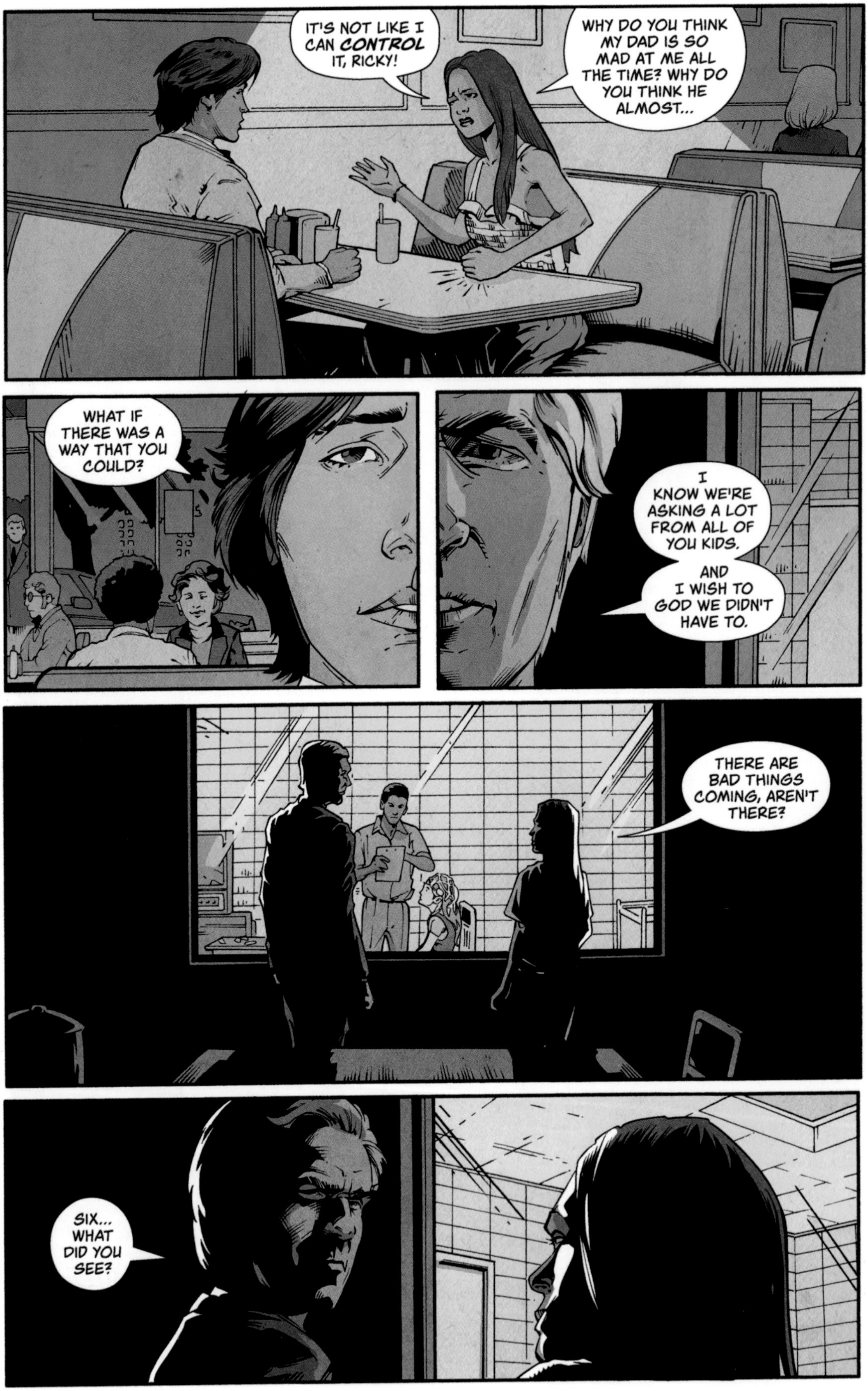
IT'S NOT LIKE I CAN *CONTROL* IT, RICKY!
WHY DO YOU THINK MY DAD IS SO MAD AT ME ALL THE TIME? WHY DO YOU THINK HE ALMOST...
WHAT IF THERE WAS A WAY THAT YOU COULD?
I KNOW WE'RE ASKING A LOT FROM ALL OF YOU KIDS.
AND I WISH TO GOD WE DIDN'T HAVE TO.
THERE ARE BAD THINGS COMING, AREN'T THERE?
SIX... WHAT DID YOU SEE?

NO,
I DIDN'T
MEAN...

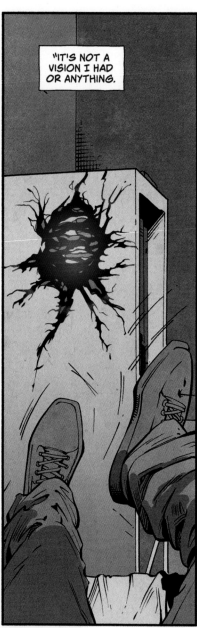

"IT'S NOT A
VISION I HAD
OR ANYTHING.

"MORE OF A
FEELING. LIKE...
SOMETHING COLD.

"SOMETHING
BAD, MAYBE."

DO YOU
KNOW WHAT
THAT COULD
BE?

NO.
I CAN'T
SAY THAT
I DO.

BUT I HAVE
A WAY WE CAN
POSSIBLY FIND OUT.
IF YOU THINK YOU'RE
READY TO TAKE THE
NEXT STEP.

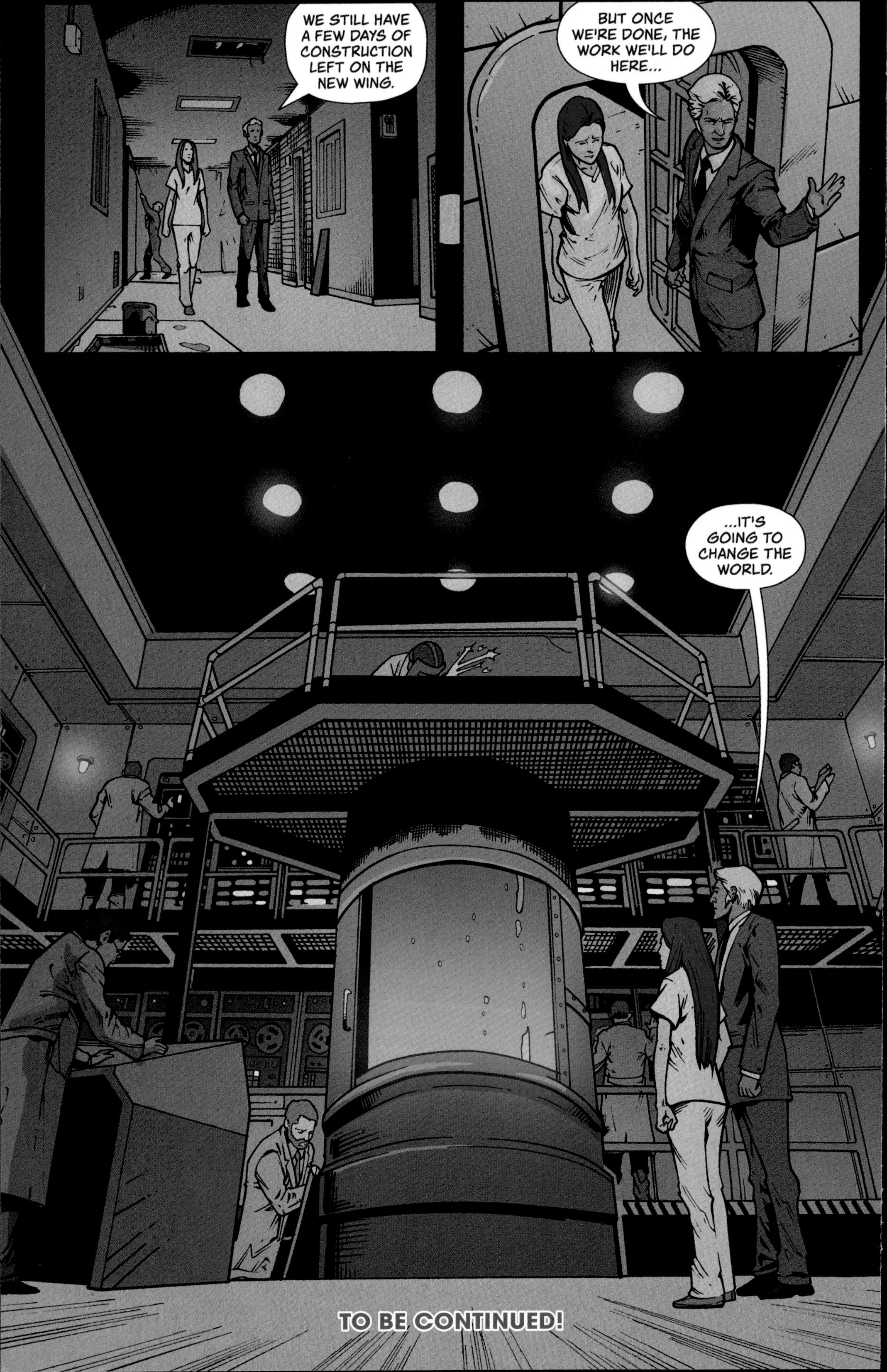
WE STILL HAVE A FEW DAYS OF CONSTRUCTION LEFT ON THE NEW WING.
BUT ONCE WE'RE DONE, THE WORK WE'LL DO HERE...
...IT'S GOING TO CHANGE THE WORLD.
TO BE CONTINUED!